LITTLE RACCOON
AND THE THING IN THE POOL

LITTLE RACCOON AND

LILIAN MOORE
PICTURES BY GIOIA FIAMMENGHI

Whittlesey House
McGraw-Hill Book Company, Inc.
New York   Toronto   London

THE THING IN THE POOL

Also by Lilian Moore
TONY THE PONY
BEAR TROUBLE

LIBRARY OF CONGRESS CATALOG CARD NUMBER: 62-16274.

PUBLISHED BY WHITTLESEY HOUSE
A DIVISION OF THE MCGRAW-HILL BOOK COMPANY, INC.

To Jean

Guy

and Jonny

Little Raccoon was little
but he was brave.

One day Mother Raccoon said,
"Tonight the moon will be
bright and full.

Can you go to the running stream
all by yourself, Little Raccoon?

Can you bring back some crayfish
for supper?"

"Oh yes, yes!" said Little Raccoon.
"I'll bring back the best crayfish
you ever ate!"

Little Raccoon was little
but he *was* brave.

That night the moon came up
big and full and very bright.

"Go now, Little Raccoon,"
said his mother.

"Walk till you come to the pool.

You will see a big tree
lying across the pool.

Walk across the pool on the tree.

The best place to dig for crayfish
is on the other side."

Little Raccoon went off
in the bright moonlight.
He was so happy
and so proud.
Here he was—
    walking in the woods
    all by himself
    for the very first time!

He walked a little.

He ran a little.

And now and then he skipped.

Soon Little Raccoon came to the place
where the tall trees grew.

There was Old Porcupine, resting.

He was surprised to see Little Raccoon
walking in the woods without his mother.

"Where are you going, all by yourself?"
asked Old Porcupine.

"To the running stream,"
said Little Raccoon proudly.

"I'm going to get some crayfish
for supper."

"Be careful, Little Raccoon,"
said Old Porcupine.
"You don't have what I have,
you know!"

"I'm not afraid,"
said Little Raccoon.
He was little,
but he was brave.

Little Raccoon went on
in the bright moonlight.

He walked a little.

He ran a little.

And now and then he skipped.

Soon he came to the place where
the sweet grass grew.

There was Big Skunk.

He was surprised, too,
to see Little Raccoon walking in the woods
without his mother.

"Where are you going, all by yourself?"
asked Big Skunk.

"To the running stream,"
said Little Raccoon proudly.

"I'm going to get some crayfish
for supper."

"Be careful, Little Raccoon,"
said Big Skunk.

"You don't have what I have,
you know!"

"I'm not afraid,"
said Little Raccoon, and he went on.

Not far from the running stream
he saw Fat Rabbit.

Fat Rabbit was sleeping, but he
opened one eye.

Then he jumped up.

"My, you scared me!" he said.

"Where are you going, Little Raccoon,
all by yourself?"

"I'm going to the running stream,"
said Little Raccoon proudly.

"Way over there on the other side
of the pool."

"OOOOOH!" said Fat Rabbit.
"Aren't you afraid of IT?"

"Afraid of what?"
asked Little Raccoon.
"Of the thing in the pool!"
said Fat Rabbit. "I am!"

"Well, I'm not!"
said Little Raccoon,
and he went on.

Soon Little Raccoon came
to the big tree that was lying
across the pool.

"This is where I cross,"
said Little Raccoon to himself.
"And over there on the other side
is where I dig for crayfish."

Little Raccoon walked on to the tree,
and began to cross the pool.

He *was* brave, but he did wish
he had not met Fat Rabbit.

He did not want to think about IT.

He did not want to think about
the thing in the pool.

But he couldn't help it.

He just had to stop—
and look.

There *was* something in the pool!

There it was, in the bright moonlight, looking up at him!

Little Raccoon did not want to show he was afraid.

So he made a face.

The thing in the pool made a face, too.

And what a mean face it was!

Little Raccoon turned and ran.

He ran past Fat Rabbit so fast
he scared him again.

He ran and ran and did not stop
till he saw Big Skunk.

"What is it?   What is it?"
asked Big Skunk.

"There's a big thing in the pool!"
said Little Raccoon.

"I can't get past it!"

"Do you want me to go with you?"
asked Big Skunk.

"I can make it go away."

"Oh no, no!"
said Little Raccoon quickly.

"You don't have to do that!"

"Well, then," said Big Skunk,
"take a stone with you.
Just show that thing in the pool
you have a stone!"

Little Raccoon did want to bring home
the crayfish.

So he took a stone, and he walked
back to the pool.

"Maybe the thing went away,"
Little Raccoon said to himself.

But no.

When he looked down into the water,
there it was!

Little Raccoon did not want to show
he was afraid.

He held up his stone.
But the thing in the pool
held up a stone, too.
And what a big stone it was!

Little Raccoon was brave
but he *was* little.

He ran like anything.

He ran and ran and he did not stop
till he saw Old Porcupine.

"What is it? What is it?"
asked Old Porcupine.

Little Raccoon told him about
the thing in the pool.

"He had a stone, too,"
said Little Raccoon.

"A big BIG stone!"

"Then you must have a stick this time,"
said Old Porcupine.

"Go back and show that you have
a big stick!"

Little Raccoon did want to bring home
the crayfish.

So he took a stick and walked back
to the pool.

"Maybe this time it went away,"
Little Raccoon said to himself.

But no.

The thing in the pool was still there.

Little Raccoon did not wait.

He held up his big stick
and shook it.

But the thing in the pool
had a stick, too.

A big **BIG** stick.

And it shook the stick at Little Raccoon.

Little Raccoon dropped his stick
and ran.
He ran and ran

past Fat Rabbit—

past Big Skunk—

past Old Porcupine—

and he did not stop till he was home.

Little Raccoon told his mother
all about the thing in the pool.
    "Oh, Mother," he said,
    "I wanted to go for crayfish
all by myself.
    I wanted to bring home our supper!"

    "And you shall!" said Mother Raccoon.
    "Go back to the pool, Little Raccoon.
But this time do not make a face.
Do not carry a stone.
Do not carry a stick."

"But what *shall* I do?"
asked Little Raccoon.

"Just smile," said Mother Raccoon.
"This time just smile at the thing
in the pool."

"Is that all?" asked Little Raccoon.
"Are you sure?"

"That is all," said his mother.
"I am sure."

Little Raccoon was brave
and his mother was sure.

So he went all the way back
to the pool again.

"Maybe the thing went away
at last," he said to himself.

But no.
There it was!
Little Raccoon made himself
stand still.
He made himself look down
into the water.

Then he made himself smile
at the thing in the pool.
The thing in the pool smiled back!

Little Raccoon was so happy
he began to laugh.

The thing in the pool seemed to laugh, too,
just like a happy raccoon.

"Now it wants to be friends,"
said Little Raccoon to himself.

"Now I can cross!"

And he ran along the tree to the other side
of the pool.

There in the running stream, Little Raccoon
began to dig.

Soon he had all the crayfish he could carry.

He ran back along the tree across the pool.
This time Little Raccoon waved
to the thing in the pool.

The thing in the pool waved back!

Little Raccoon went home with the crayfish as fast as he could go.

It was the best crayfish he and Mother Raccoon ever ate.

Mother Raccoon said so, too.

"I can go by myself any time now,"
said Little Raccoon.

"I'm not afraid of the thing
in the pool now."

"I know," said Mother Raccoon.

"The thing in the pool isn't
mean at all!" said Little Raccoon.

"I know," said Mother Raccoon.

Little Raccoon looked at his mother.
"Tell me," he said.
"What *is* the thing in the pool?"

Mother Raccoon began to laugh.
Then she told him.

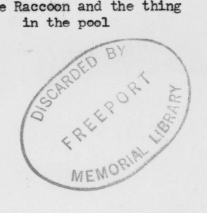
Freeport Memorial Library
FREEPORT, N. Y.
Juvenile Department

All books may be kept for two weeks, and
may be renewed once for the same period.

Books may be renewed by mail or telephone.

One cent a day is charged for all overdue
books.

Each borrower is held responsible for all
books and magazines drawn on his card, and
for all fines accruing on the same.

FREEPORT MEMORIAL LIBRARY